WORKING FOR THE SUBBY

(JOHNJO'S TALE)

By

Tom O'Brien

first printing

Published by tomtom-theatre

WORKING FOR THE SUBBY
(Johnjo's tale)

You can never go back, they say. And maybe they're right. They can't stop you going back in your mind though. And right now mine has me sitting on a hill, looking down on some windswept, craggy fields. In the distance I can see the faint outlines of farm buildings. Our farm buildings.

Come all ye loyal heroes wherever you may be

Don't hire with any Master till you know what your work will be

For you must rise up early from the clear daylight till dawn

Or else you won't be able to plough the Rocks of Bawn

My father was always singing bits of that song. I don't know, maybe he didn't know any more of it, but those are the only words that stick in my mind. I suppose, though, they had a certain ring...Plough...Rocks...Bawn....I mean, look at it...More rocks than bawn...

By God, if I had a penny for every stone we picked...For every furze bush we cut down.

I can still hear him now:

'Fifty acres, boy...and five of them is a hill. What good is a lump of limestone to a farmer? You can't feed beasts on rocks. By God, if I had my way, I'd blast the whole lot to kingdom come...'

Then he'd be off singing again

I am a little beggar man and begging I have been

For three score and more in this little isle of green

With me sikidder-e-idle- di And me skidder-e-idle-do

Everybody knows me by the name of Johnny Rhu.

That was his favourite song He would sometimes sit me on his knee, and while he was reaching behind him trying to locate the drop of poteen hidden under the rock, we would hear my mother calling;

' Johhny, Johnny where are you? Out there in the cold with the child! Come on in now and milk the cows...'

'Shh…we'll be as quiet as two mice, boy…'

He would locate the poteen and take a good mouthful, then rub some on my lips.

'Better than mother's milk, that is...'

Then he would tell me one of his stories

'Did I ever tell you about the time Finn Macool picked up The Giants Causeway and threw it into the sea? He huffed and he puffed, and he humped and he jumped...

Anyway, he finally managed to get a hould of the Causeway in his arms and he heaved it into the water. And do you know why? So he could walk all the way to Scotland.'

Then he would laugh. 'Twas a long way to go for a job...'

The laugh would get mother going again.

'Johnny...what ould rubbish are you filling his head with now...?'

He'd wait until she stopped.

'All quiet on the western front again. Your mother is like Epsom Salts...best taken in small doses. De Valera is up there now, boy. Sittin' on the throne. The one he's always wanted. I only hope he knows what he's doing. Up Dev.'

That would set her off again.

'You and your 'Up Dev'. When he gives us the extra land that he promised, then you can sing all about...Mr De Valera.'

'Have no fear, Dev is here...'

'Come down from there you drunken fool. And bring the child with you.'

Course the extra land never materialised. Politicians don't change, do they? Oh, some got a few acres here and there. Maybe they knew Dev's mother-in-law, or bought an ass from his cousin. But most, like my father, got sweet fuck-all. Mind you, Jackie Nugent over in Carrickbeg got some. 'How much?', I heard my father ask him one day. 'Fifteen acres', he says...'when the tide is out'

You don't mind if I take a sip of this, do you? I like a drop of diesel. I always have. There's no harm in having a little of what you fancy. Or a lot.

You can see three counties from here. That's Tipperary over there... Up Tipp!

And there's Kilkenny. Ah, Kilkenny...

> And in Kilkenny it is reported
>
> They have marble stones as black as ink
>
> With gold and silver I will support her
>
> But I'll sing no more now till I get a drink..

Up the Black and Amber, boys! And them's the Comeragh Mountains there...see? If I reach out I can almost touch them. And up there...look! Crotty's Eye. That's where Crotty, the highwayman used to hide, waiting for his chance to rob the poor feckers passing by below.

I might have been a highwayman in different times. Well, why not? Not much for disenfranchised young Irishmen to do in those days, was there? Not like Crotty, though.

He was stupid; he got hung for his trouble in Waterford City.

The English...they loved hanging Irish people. Still do, given half a chance, I expect.

And there, see...that's Croughamore...all two thousand acres of it. You can just pick out Croughamore House. See...over there, where those trees are...well, what's left of it, anyway. There's no rocks in Croughamore. Least not unwanted ones.

And the grass is so sweet the cows bellies are almost touching the ground...

And Lord Croughamore - or whatever his title was - was an English bastard, born and bred.

D'you mind if I take another drink?

Burn everything British, 'cept their coal - that's what I say...

The Big House, that's what we called it Everyone did. It stood for something. A symbol.

Of...everything English. I would come up herewith father and watch him look at it with loathing. We used to throw stones at it...and it two miles away for fuck sake!

I can hear him again:

'See that place, boy? Your ancestors and my ancestors were thrun off that land by his ancestors. Never forget that. Put out on to the side of the road, and their biteen of ahouse sent tumbling down behind them There was nearly fifty families received the same treatment...all tenant-farmers like our-selves. Mind you, they **did** get two pounds each in compensation...

And what was it all in aid of? Greed, boy. The more land they had, the more they wanted.

Not that it's changed much since...Land does something to a man...affects his brain. Men have been known to kill for a bit of ould bog.

Look at the range wars in America...and the wiping out of the Indians and the buffalos...wasn't that only about one thing? Land.

And when countries invade other countries...what's that about only land?

Ah Jesus, boy, I wish I had some land...real land. And when I had it, I'd let no...bastard take it away.'

He was never going to get it...not that he'd know what do with it, anyway. He was a farmer in name only; by nature he was a......I'd say he was a throwback to the Tuatha De Dannan. Able to do many things well...but not farming. He could tell stories; he could sing; he could dance.

Of all the trades a going, sure begging is the best

When a man is tired, he can sit down and rest

He can beg for his dinner, he has nothing else to

But to slip around the corner with his old rigadoo

Mother knew him only too well; I suppose that's why she kept on at him. Who knows what he might have done if she hadn't? The only thing she couldn't control was the poteen and the Woodbines. He'd smoke Woodbines till the cows come home.

Then the war came and everything was rationed. He'd cycle into Town every now and again.

' Fifteen miles!' she would say. 'Fifteen miles for a fag, and you wouldn't walk half a mile down the road to get a loaf of bread for the table.'

Sometimes he'd be gone for days and I would be sent to find him.

He was usually down by the quay, watching the ships coming and going.

On the rocks...high up. I was always afraid he might fall in...

'And who'd miss me if I did?' he would ask, before taking another drink

> I'm a rambler I'm a gambler, I'm a long way from home
>
> And if you don't like me just leave me alone
>
> I'll eat when I'm hungry, and I'll drink when I'm dry
>
> And if moonshine don't kill me I'll live till I die.

I often thought he was thinking about...you know, jumping...but I never let on to mother...

Everything seemed to be going okay until the day we heard the sound of a plane overhead. He got very excited and dragged me with him to the highest point on the hill

'Come on, boy! That's a German plane, if ever I heard one...'

And he's away, making firing noises all over the place, running this way and that.

'That's it...that's your target... the Big House...you can't miss it...'

In his excitement, he tripped over a rock, and crashed head-first into a bigger one.

He lays there, blood pumping from his head. Somehow, I knew it was over.

' Daddy! Daddy! Don't die. Please don't die...'

I cradled him in my arms as his life ebbed away and the only thing I could think of was that he had never told me he loved me

... ……………………..

'Johnjo! Come on down from there. You have things to do in the morning.'

I had indeed. I was taking our last remaining bullock to Buckley's level-crossing...putting him on the train, and taking him to the market in Dungarvan ten miles away

Everyone was sorry for my trouble. I was myself. But the time for sorrow was over. Life had to go on. And the funeral had to be paid for...

'Twenty eight pounds ten, twenty nine...and ten shillings for luck...'

I had twenty eight pounds and ten shillings in my back pocket, and the bullock was heading in the Cork direction. I got the bus back to the village, went round to the undertaker and paid him his twenty three pounds. Then I called on the parish priest and gave him his three pounds for the funeral service and the Mass. When I got home, I gave my mother the two pounds ten shillings I had left. She said it was all we had between us and the poorhouse.

I wasn't long changing all that.

It was something father had said...another one of his stories.

   Francis Wyse, a self-righteous bastard of a landlord...oh back in the time of the famine...had evicted all of his tenants the day after they finished the harvest. Not the day before, mind – the day after. Anyway, they all ganged-up and stormed the place a few nights afterwards, shouting; 'your corn or your life'. They cleaned the place out.

Your corn or your life!

I need another sup of this diesel.

Nothing so dramatic for me. I was green but I wasn't gormless. Just the odd sheep. There was a butcher I'd heard about in Dungarvan who wasn't too particular where his supply came from. And it was always cash up front.

Occasionally he'd kill one for me. I'd salt it and store it for our own use. Me and Ma.

I know what you're thinking...stealing from people no better off than myself.

No, that wasn't it.

Croughamore House, that's where I got them. They had so many they'd never miss a few. Least that's what I thought...

Isn't it funny how a few shillings in your pocket changes your outlook on life?

You could go to the pictures...a dance...maybe have a few jars in a pub...

You think I was a bit young for the pub?

I looked older than my age...and to be honest, they weren't too fussy.

Carrick - where I used to go - was like a ghost town as far as men were concerned.

I suppose the war had a lot to do with it. Even though it was an English war, a lot of Irishmen were fighting in it.

But it was the times as well; there was no work. Dev's vision of a homely, self-sufficient nation was a joke - and those who weren't off fighting were over in England working in the factories and on the farms...sending home money to their families - when they thought of it.

And places like Carrick were full of women looking for a man. Any man. A young fella of seventeen was in great demand...

One of the hotels used to run dances, and was so short of men, they used to send the barman out in an old Transit van. Round-up time, he called it.

It was the beginning of a life-long association between me and the back of Transit vans.

A lot of the time it was all innocent fun; a few drinks a few dances- and if it wasn't always like that, sure, isn't that what made the world go round.

There was one song that always got me going at the dances.

Flow on lovely river, flow gently along

By your waters so sweet sound the larks merry song

On your green banks I wonder there first I did join

With you lovely Molly The rose of Mooncoin.

Another of my father's songs. And whenever I heard it sung everything would well up inside me. He had been singing it in the field as we rebuilt a stone wall just minutes before the German plane came into sight. I never knew what that plane was doing in our vicinity, but I guess the pilot must have got lost. He was certainly well off the mark if his target was London or the South Coast of England, and I guess if he hadn't strayed then father wouldn't have died like that. A casualty of war is how it would be described I suppose, though in my book German stupidity had something to do with it.

Everyone called me Blondie now. Well, I was as blonde as a...Viking. Maybe I was a Viking...not my father's son at all. I mean...when I thought about it - and I was thinking about it a lot more lately - there wasn't much resemblance.

What was it I read somewhere?

'The natives are ugly, squat people, with low foreheads...'.

That was him to a tee...Looking back on it now, I remember him looking at me out of the corner of his eye sometimes...sizing me up. I suppose he was wondering the same as I was.

At first it was great. Women all over me. And drink. I wasn't getting home till all hours. Mother knew something was going on...but I think she was too afraid to ask. I said I was helping the butcher out, to account for the money. Well, he had an ould slaughter-house the other side of the hill...I think it half convinced her.

She had this idea in her head: we'd sell the farm and move into Town, and she'd buy a shop. I'd be able to get a decent job, and after a while, I could take over in the shop. There was one flaw; there were no jobs – decent or otherwise. And if there were, what was I qualified for? Apart from making piles of rocks? Anyway, I wanted to see a bit of the world. Somewhere that didn't remind me of a hill farm. I had already made up my mind;

Oh Mary this London's a wonderful sight

Where the people are working by day and by night

They don't sow potatoes or barley or wheat

But there's gangs of them digging for gold in the street.

I was off to England as soon as I could get a few more shillings together. And pluck up the courage to tell her!

It was St Patricks night, and everyone had been wetting the shamrock since early in the day; singing, dancing and generally acting the eejit. I went to watch the Parade in town - they had a band and marching girls down from Down. Down from Down!

Anyway, I bumped into the butcher... Wet the shamrock? We drowned it! And in the course of it I outlined my plan.

 I would...liberate ten sheep from The Big House - well, who would take a blind bit of notice on St Paddy's night? - and drive them to his slaughterhouse.

The rest was up to him. He hummed and he hawed - I thought he was a bit off-hand to be honest - but in the end he agreed. There was only one little problem; I would have to wait a couple of days for my money.

Have you ever tried to drive sheep in the dark? Well, not completely dark; there was a bit of a moon, but the state I was in wasn't helping things...

How's ever, I managed it. Well, five sheep anyway. That's all I had left by the time I got to the shed. That's all his slaughterhouse was...a big bloody shed.

I expected the door to be open – and it was. What I wasn't expecting was the reception when I drove the sheep inside...They were waiting for me; O'Shea, the farm manager, and two others who I didn't recognise.

It was a set-up.

I can still hear that fucker O'Shea

'By jaysus, McGrath, by the time we're finished with you, you'll wish you hadn't been born. I suppose you think you are carrying on a long line of tradition. Your father's gone, and now it's your turn. Your sheep-stealing father.They hung sheep-stealers not so long ago. How would you like to be strung up like your ancestors? Your fucking sheep-stealing ancestors?'

I wasn't waiting to find out how I would like it. Christ! I felt like I was going to choke. I could feel the rope tightening around my neck as he spoke. There was bench with several butchers knives...I grabbed one and made a run for it...Somehow...I don't know how - I think they must have stepped back when they saw the knife - I was through the door. Then I realised there was blood everywhere...and when I turned round O'Shea was lying there in the moonlight, the knife sticking out of him...I don't know...I must'a seen red...It was all a blur... My father as a sheep-stealer? He never stole anything in his life...I must'a just...just...

I cleaned up myself as best I could in the stream, then I went home, put a few things in a bag, put the few shilling I had saved in my pocket, and woke mother.

I can hear her now;

'Ah, Johnjo, don't go. Johnjo, why? Why must you go...?'

I couldn't tell her why. She'd find out soon enough.

'How's she cutting, Blondie...?

'Hey Blondie, get your arse over here and get the beers in...'

Oh the crack was good in Cricklewood

But t'was better in the Crown

There was bottles flying and Biddies crying

And Paddies going to town...

'Are you goin' home for the Christmas, Blondie…?

Home for Christmas? I hadn't been home for more than thirty years...

What's that saying? You can never go back -unless you have a hundred pounds

in your pocket....or haven't a charge of attempted murder hanging over you.

What's the statute of limitations for that now?

I was a wanted man.

I almost expected to see my picture on wanted posters.

You know…like Jesse James or Billy The Kid...

WANTED -DEAD OR ALIVE - JONJO MCGRATH -ALIAS BLONDIE.
LAST SEEN HEADING FOR LINCOLNSHIRE....

Why Lincolnshire? I don't know. It was farming country; I read somewhere there was loads of work going there. And I thought I might be well away from Mr Hitler's doodlebugs. I was - and so were a lot of others...

Wealthy Englishmen who had bought up a lot of the farms in the area - with the sole intention of keeping their sons out of the war...

Doing their bit for their country?...Hah! They knew fuck all about farming. That's why they hired eejits like me...
They treated us like shit. We had to live in stables and haylofts. Working all hours. Picking spuds...muck-spreading...milking...harvesting...you name it. We had no names.It was Paddy this...Paddy that...Paddy you thick cunt. The prisoners-of-war were treated better than us But what could I do? I was on the run. And to make matters worse I had to report to the local police station every three months. Otherwise I could be deported. I was bollixed whichever way I turned...

Oh, the praties they were small over here

The praties they were small over here

The praties they were small

But we ate them skins and all

They were better than fuck all over here...

There's Big Houses wherever you go in the world. And people to go with them

Did you ever heartell of Elephant John? No not the Elephant Man.

Mind you, he **was** an ugly fucker, I will say that. Not that his looks held him back; when you look at all the millions he has now you might even conclude that his looks were his fortune. The right mixture of brawn and brain, I guess. Well, what else? We both started off on the same level – and look at him now.

He has a lot to answer for... Elephant John. I suppose he was a trend setter of his time. Setting a style in fashions that thousands followed. The badly-undressed look, I guess you would call it…

>Just take a stroll through Cricklewood or Kilburn

>You'll recognise him half a mile away

>On his backside is tattooed the map of Ireland

>And a big black wart stands out on Galway bay...

Elephant John had a lot in common with Finn McCool. He could move mountains...or mountains of muck anyway. Trouble was, he expected everyone else to do the same. Stuck you down a hole in the morning, and expected it to be an underground car-park in the evening. The subbies friend, until he became one himself.

Mind you, there were plenty more like him. Re-building England...what was left of it after Mr Hitler had finished. I didn't hang around Lincolnshire too long after the fighting was over. I'd had enough of those bastards. And as for the police...I thought I'd keep them in the dark too. I might as well be hung for a lamb as a sheep!

Building the motorways kept me busy. And we were always on the move - which suited me. We lived in camps you wouldn't keep a decent dog in. And with fellas like Elephant John dogging you day and night, I often felt I had jumped from the frying pan into the fire. But I was free.
You know...FREE. Whatever that meant.

You know the great American Dream? Life, liberty, and freedom for all...Or something like that.

Well, this was the Irish version...Work, drudgery, and sweet fuck all.

BUT I WAS FREE.

We played cards to pass the time. Ah jaysus, I was a martyr for the cards. Thirty and forty five...

'Hey, Blondie, you reneged that one...'

'Tray of spades...I led the tray of spades...'

'Ah Jaysus lads, can't someone stop the jink...'

You could lose your week's wages in one night. And some of us did. Then you'd be stuck in the camp for the weekend, the lucky ones living it up in Kiburn and Cricklewood at your expense.

'Take your partners for a Seige Of Ennis...'

The Buffalo...The Galtymore....The Banba ...We rubbed bellies in all of them.

The Banba.... where they held a tea-dance on Sunday afternoons- and us drunken Paddies went to sober up for the night ahead. Or fought running battles with members of the Sunshine Gang, who saw that particular stretch of the Kilburn High Road as their exclusive territory.

They say that behind every drunken Irishman is a sober Irish woman...and all trying to wean their fella off the bottle. I suppose it's true. All those doe-eyed colleens slaving away in the sweatshops of Kilburn and Cricklewood during the week; McVities, Heinz, Smiths, Staples; and looking for love in the Galty at the weekend. Keeping their legs so tight together that jackhammers couldn't prise them apart...
If marriages were made in heaven, they were negotiated in places like the Galty...

And if you wanted to get your leg over, you had to put a roof over their heads first.Maybe that's why I never...took the plunge. I never cared for the game in the first place.

But there were other...considerations.

Not least of them being that I was now living in a totally male environment. There were no women digging holes for McAlpines or Murphys. At least I never saw any. And I was quite happy for it to be that way.

If you get my drift.

There was no big revelation. No big dawning. I just kind of...drifted into it .Weekends at the camp. There were others like me...Ah, fuck it - I wound up sleeping with men...

I liked sleeping with men...

I still do...

It was better than sticking it in a sheep -like I saw plenty do in the wilds of Lincolnshire and Bedfordshire. And so what?

It was no big fucking deal. And it's my business, anyway.

The other thing that put the kybosh on marriage -oh aye, it was still in the back of my mind then, get married and have children - was the fact that I was on the run. In two countries.

There was no future for anyone with me. Unless I was prepared to give myself up. And that was one thing I wasn't planning on.

I was thinking afterwards, that if I had killed that fucker O'Shea, and had been convicted, I could have been swinging from the gallows in Kilmainham before the year was out.

Hang down your head Tom Dooley

Hang down your head and cry

Hang down your head Tom Dooley.
Poor boy you're gonna die

Poor boy you're gonna die...

When the lads first started calling me Tom, I'd be looking around to see who they were talking to. Well, I couldn't use my real name, could I? So Tom Dooley it was. Mind you, most were calling me Blondie soon enough.

It was great gas, seeing the names going down on the worksheet on a morning. Robin Hood. Gene Autry. Donald Duck. Even Nelson Rockerfellar.

'And what's your name?', the subby asked one fella

'Sammy Davis Junior', came the reply

'Where have you come from?'

'Holyhead'.

'Oh aye. And where are you heading... Hollywood?'.

Some of them should have been actors. Hollywood navvies, we called them. You know the type; designer wellies, shirts off at the first hint of a bit of sun. You'd know, in the back of the Transit, after the first day, that they wouldn't be back...

Ah, the crack was mighty then...

You don't mind if I have another of these...?

Whenever I had a few shillings to spare, I'd send it to my mother. I used to get one of the lads to post the letters, all from different places.

You couldn't trust any of those fuckers back home; The Gardai, the Post Office, they're all the same. They could be steaming open the letters...how the fuck would you know?

And then I heard of a way.

You could have letters sent to you, addressed to a named post office. It was called post restaurant or something.

I took my friend, Fergal, along the first time. Well, if they were waiting, and they picked him up, they'd soon find out he wasn't me.

I needn't have worried. I was investing them with qualities they didn't possess...

Oh, don't let the cut of me fool you. I mightn't have went to school, but I met the scholars - as they say.

Then I had a letter from Ma:

Dear Johnjo,

Are you ever coming home again? That was an awful thing you did to Mr O'Shea, and he married with five childer. He was in hospital for six months. Sergeant Foley says it would be best if you gave yourself up. He says he'd speak for you. Mind you, I wouldn't trust that fecker to spit straight. The bank is being very good, letting me have money and all. I told them it might be a while before we could pay it back, but they said not to worry. Wasn't that nice? I don't do much these days, but Jim Foley, the butcher, the one you used to do the bit of work for, has taken some of the land for grazing for his sheep. They say he got them cheap from the Big House....

Got them cheap! The slimy bastard...!

I suppose I should have gone home, took the medicine, as they say. But what good could I do mother in goal? Besides, I was afraid of what I might do - to certain people...you know?

After about six or seven years the letters stopped. Just like that. When six months had gone by I knew something was up, and I was thinking maybe I should sneak home - just to see what was going on.

Then one more letter arrived. It was official-looking, so I knew it was bad news.

To Mr John McGrath, or his representatives; Over a period of time, we advanced your mother sums of money against her property at Knockbawn. Since her death last year, we have been unable to see any return on our investment, and have now foreclosed on the mortgage. The land is now the property of the bank, and will be sold by public auction in due course. Should you wish to negotiate re-purchase of the property, you may of course do so any time before the auction date...

Since her death last year...!

That was the first I heard of it. I know she drowned herself. Oh the inquest said it was accidental, but I know different. She couldn't swim a stroke, so what was she doing out swimming? And why Clonea Strand? She never went there. We never went there. It was always Bonmahon.

Do you know how I found out how she died? I hired a private detective

The Acme Detective Agency. I'm not making it up. It was the only way I could think of...

I think he thought I was mad. But what did I care?

> In Dixieland I take my stand
>
> To live and die in Dixie
>
> 'Cause Dixieland,
>
> That's where I was born
>
> Early Lord one frosty morn
>
> Look away, look away
>
> Look away, Dixieland

They fuck you up, don't they? People I mean. I don't mean my mother and father. I fucked them up. Well, my mother anyway. The way I left her like that. My father was always fucked up. In the conventional sense. He didn't conform, you see. I mean...a farmer who didn't farm. You can see how it looked to others.

He wasn't a fucking sheep-stealer!

I fucked up. That's what I did. I fucked up my whole life. I mean, who am I? Look at me!

I'm not Blondie. Not any more. Am I Johnjo McGrath?

Who is Johnjo McGrath?

Who am I?

I have a library card that say Tom Dooley. It's got my signature. That proves it's me. That's the only bit of paper I have with my name on it.

A bloody library card!

I don't exist officially

I never have.

Yet I got by.

No tax, no insurance, no driving licence.

Never paid any. Never had any.

Yet I got by.

I was fifty last year. Or is it this? See how difficult it is when you're...

Certain dates stick in the mind. But not my own birthday.

John Fitzgerald Kennedy: Dallas, Texas, November the twenty-third, nineteen-sixty-three. I well remember where I was that day. I was up to my goolies in shite, digging a trench for Mr Bannaher. But then, I was most days.

July the twentieth, nineteen-sixty-nine, when Neil Armstrong first walked on the moon, where was I? Up to my goolies in shite, digging a trench for Mr Bannaher. But then, I was most days...

If you listen closely you can hear the sound Transit van revving up in the distance, and shouts and laughter coming from inside. It's half past six on a frosty March morning, and most of Kilburn is turning over for its second sleep. And us lucky ones are all aboard the Orange Blossom Special, calling Kilburn, Cricklewood, Hendon, Watford, and all stations south of the Gap...

'Jump in there, Blondie. I see you spent another night looking at the stars'.

'But not from the gutter. Ah...you're nothing but a shower of tinkers. I'll have you know I slept the night in a grand warm bed. Mrs McGinty. She keeps lovely rooms. Round the back of the Elephant'

'You slept at the foot of the fucking Elephant, pissed as a fart!'

'I'll have you know that not a drop of alcohol has passed my lips for a fortnight now...

'You must be dying for a dhrop then. Here...'

> 'Twas down the glen came Bannaher's men
>
> Like a troop of Bengal lancers
>
> One in ten were time-served men
>
> The rest were fucking chancers.

The mystery tour, we called it. Arses plonked in the back of that Transit van, then off to God-knows- where. Heads down, arses up for the rest of the day, up to your goolies in muck.

'Hey Blondie! Are you pulling that cable or what?

'Leave him alone, he's pulling his wire'

'Keep the big mixer going, boys'.

After pulling Bannaher's wire all day, you wouldn't be in much form for pulling your own that night. Or anyone else's. A few pints in the Crown or the Nags Head, then back to a damp room - if you were lucky. And nothing to look forward to the next day except more of the same. And the day after that.All pissed up against the pub walls. Left in the clubs and betting shops of Kilurn and Cricklewood...

Isn't the craving an awful affliction? I do see men in the morning and they on fire for a sup of the craythur. That fire do be burning all your life. It's what keeps you down that damp hole. What keeps you putting your hand out to men like Bannaher. 'A sub, a sub, my soul for a sub'. That's what you do. You sell your soul to the subby. Well, who else would want it. Sure isn't that where we lord it over the English? We can breed bigger and more ignorant bastards than they can, any day of the week. Bastards like Bannaher. And to cap it all, we're all in here...in the bar of the...Heartbreak Hotel, propping it up, or being propped up, falling over each other to ingratiate ourselves with the Big Man. You could understand all the forelock-tugging and arse-licking if he was a Sassanach - after all, we've had centuries of practice – but a jumped-up bogman with the skid-marks still showing...

They're happy...They're fucking happy!

Some say the devil is dead,

The devil is dead, the devil is dead

Some say the devil is dead

And buried in Killarney

More say he rose again,

Rose again, rose again

More say he rose again

And joined the British Army.

'Shut up Duggan, you ould bollix!'

That's Dougie. Another of Bannahers wire-pullers. He's on a special assignment at present. Instead of digging one of Bannahers holes, he's buried in one. In a coffin. In the back garden of the pub. Oh, it's only a temporary arrangement. We hope. And it's all for a good cause. Charity.

At least that's the official line.

I asked Dougie if he was doing it for charity and he nearly choked himself laughing. 'Charity me hole! I'm getting five hundred quid off Bannaher for it'.

I only hope he asked for his five hundred in advance.

I mean, look at him. Look at the Big Man. The crease on them trousers is so sharp you could cut yourself... I can see what's in it for him, of course. The publicity. When he bought this place a few months ago, there were more pigeons than customers. Look at it now! He's even got his own tame bank manager. Every Friday evening. Changing cheques. Five percent. Oh, it's big business. Well, how many the likes of me have bank accounts? Or would want one? It was easy in the old days - cash in the paw and no questions asked.

And they're his own cheques for fuck sake!

He pays you by cheque, then charges five percent to change the fucking thing! And most of it finds its way back over the counter again before the weekend is out...
That's why, come Monday morning, you'll find us out there again, bleary-eyed and broke, looking for a start. And more importantly, looking for a sub. Anything to tide us over till next pay day.

I'm too old now, to lie next to anyone. And, to be honest, I don't want to anymore. Keep myself to myself, that's my motto. And play with myself too. It's less...taxing. There was a time when I was in demand. Blondie was in demand...big time. Ah, but what can't be cured must be endured, as someone once said. Besides, there's no one I would want to...with...anymore.

You'll excuse me am moment now while I...

A bit of shuttering, that's all it wanted. A bit of fucking shuttering...

'Oh Christ, Fergal, hang on under there...I'm digging, boy...I'm digging...oh Jesus...I'm digging...'

I gave Fergal the kiss of life, but I knew it was too late.

And do you know what that pointy-toed fucker, Bannaher, had said a few days before? 'I'm paying you pair to dig a trench, not put up shuttering'.

They should have put that on Fergal's gravestone.

All for the want of a bit of shuttering.

And now he's after twisting the knife a bit more.

'I think now, Blondie, you're getting too old for this game'.

Too old…!

Sure, maybe he's right. It's a young man's game...

But not some young men.

'How's she cutting, Terry? Terry now, he's a different generation. No better educated, but he has a different outlook...

'I'd rather starve than work on the fucking buildings'...that's his outlook.

Not that he ever would.

Starve.

Or work.

'London's a great place for people who don't like getting out of bed in the morning', says he to me once.

The time of the first race dictates when he gets out of bed.

He's steal the cross off an ass's back, that fella. He's just after doing eighteen months inside. They deported him, but he's back again.

'Looking for work, Terry?' I says to him the other day.

'Maybe', he says

'Bannaher's big mixer, is it?'

'You must be fucken joking', he said. 'I have plans that will put Bannaher in the ha-penny place'.

Well, so have I.

He comes from near me at home...Terry. Not that he knows it of course. Or that I would ever dream of telling him.
He tells me that Bannaher has bought the Big House. He probably got it for a song. It was falling down, anyway. Crows flying in and out of it. Lord what's-his-fucking-name long gone .Lord Croughamore. I think the IRA put the wind up him. A few bullets through his dining room window one night spoiling his after-dinner port.

Terry is a mine of information.

'There's an ould hill farm next door he bought too, that he's turning into a concrete batching-plant. Well the hill bit anyway. They say he's going to make a fortune out of it. Ah, it's been derelict for years. No one would buy it or go near it. They say it's haunted. A weird family lived there.

Apparently, the father hung himself and the mother drowned herself. And the son...well he stabbed several people in a fight, and was never seen again. Mind you, he must have been the weirdest of the lot because afterwards they found all these blond wigs in his room...

Ah, maybe it was all made up though. It all happened a long time ago...'

That's the story he told me. 'Course I didn't tell him my story...

I always wanted to see Nashville And The Grand Ole Opry; Roy Acuff. Bill Munro, Patsy Cline.

From The Great Atlantic Ocean

To the wide Pacific shore

From the queen of the flowing mountains

To the south bell by the door...

Look at him there behind the bar. In his counting house. Ill wipe that fucking smirk off your face...

'Hey, Bannaher, were you ever in Nashville? I was thinking of goin' there one day soon.

And I was thinking you might like to come too. What?…I can't hear ya. Stand back there Terry will ya – and let the dog see the rabbit….'

'Jaysus, Blondie, that's a fine chest you have there'

'What's that yoke with all the wires? Is that your pacemaker?'

'For Christ sakes can't ye see it's dynamite.   Ah Jesus Blondie, no! Run for it, lads!

end

11386190R00021

Printed in Great Britain
by Amazon